A POTPOURRI OF POETRY/LYRICS

A POTPOURRI OF POETRY/LYRICS

Before the Evening Ends

Volume 1

On

Love, Life, & Death

MICHAEL R. JENNINGS

DEDICATION

For Leo F Sicklebower, Jr.
US 82nd Airborne, December 24,1965

This set of poems/lyrics/songs is dedicated to Leo Sicklebower, for whom I wrote the poem/lyrics/song (**Boots on a Cross**). Of course, I have to thank Tom Austin & Julie Powers for creating the music. I wrote this poem/lyrics just prior to his 50th anniversary of being killed (KIA) in South America, Dominican Republic to be exact. As they always say, "The good always die young."

FOREWORD

This collection of Poetry/Lyrics (Volume I) is a culmination of years of imagination ... even going back to when I was eighteen-years-old. Where spelled out, it directs one to my website where a reader can, if one chooses, listen to the songs, including (mostly) my own music, where one can listen to some of recordings that I had done professionally by other singers.

INDEX OF POETRY

WHEN I GENTLY CLOSE YOUR DOOR

When you awake my child
I will be gone
For the time has come
When I must start anew
A life not meant for one
Yes, when you awake
I will be gone
Where gentle summer winds
Will blow no more
Where a child in my arms
Will be but a memory
Yes, I will be gone
To a place where my tomorrows
Will be filled with your sorrows
Sorrows that will begin anew
When I gently close your door

Yes, when you awake
I will be gone
For your mommy and I
Have come to see life
Through different eyes

Now I must go
To an unknown world
Filled with loneliness
Now I must go
To live in a world
A world without you

Sweet dreams little angel
As you lie there in your bed
Sweet dreams little angel
Innocence upon your face
Sweet dreams little angel
For when you awake
I will be gone

No longer will I see
The early morning suns
Dancing through your hair
No longer will I be
The one to dry your tears
Or chase away the ghost
That may fill your dreams
Fill your dreams at night
No longer will I hear
Your prayers before you sleep
Or your waking "I love yous"

Yes, when you awake my child
I will be gone
For the time has come
When I must start anew
A life not meant for one
Yes, when you awake
I will be gone
Where gentle summer winds
Will blow no more
Where a child in my arms
Will be but a memory

Yes, I will be gone
To a place where my tomorrows
Will be filled with your sorrows
Sorrows that will begin anew
When I gently close your door.

WAITING IN THE WINGS

Every time I take a walk
To clear my mind
Every time I seek to free
The burdens of my heart
I can't help but see
See your lovely face
Smiling warm on me
Every time within my mind
I can't help but feel
Feel your tender touch
Upon my yearning soul
A touch I used to know
In a loved filled past
But now -
When I see your face
Within my mind
Like a thunderstorm
The tears begin to fall
Yes - like a raging river free
The tears they do fall

But then I will go on
Go on loving you
'Till you return

To my loving arms
Waiting in the wings
'Till you return
Always loving you

'Till there's no more love
No more love to give
Waiting in the wings
'Till you return
'Till my dying breath
I will always love you
'Till you return
I shall forever remain
Waiting for you
Waiting in the wings
The wings of your love

I still remember when
I was on your mind
Each and every day
When there was a time
When we shared fine wine
By a single candle's flame
Yes - I remember a time
Like it was yesterday
Before you went away
When our love was grand
When love took up our nights

Yes - I remember when
I was the only one
You said you would ever love

But here I am
Laying all alone
As you're loving someone else
But yes - I will go on
Go on loving you

'Till you return
To my loving arms
Waiting in the wings
'Till you return
Always loving you
'Till there's no more love
No more love to give
Waiting in the wings
The wings of your love
'Till you return
'Till my dying breath
I will always love you
'Till you return
I shall forever remain
Waiting for you
Waiting in the wings
Waiting - Waiting
Waiting in the wings
The wings of your love

DOORWAY OF TEARS

There you were
Standing by the door
Suitcase on the floor
Yes, there you were
Tears in your eyes
Standing by the door
Ready to walk
Ready to run
To another love
To another dream
That doesn't include me
Yes, you were standing there
Standing by the doorway of tears

Through the ups and downs
Despite all the pains
That came along our way
I never once gave up
On our vows of love
I never once gave up
Throughout all the storms
That have rocked our hearts
On our way through life
Yes - Despite the pains

From all the storms
You're still the only one
I'll ever want to love
Yes, the only one
To keep this flame alive
This flame that burns for you

But there you were
Standing by the door
Suitcase on the floor
Yes, there you were
Tears in your eyes
Standing by the door
Ready to walk
Ready to run
To another love
To another dream
That doesn't include me
Yes, you were standing there
Standing by the doorway of tears

When you walk out that door
I want you to know
That you are leaving behind
One lonely broken heart
That you are leaving behind
These shattered dreams
Lying on the floor

Lying beneath your feet
Yes, these shattered dreams
A broken heart
Given to known fears
At the doorway of tears

But there you were
Standing by the door
Suitcase on the floor
Yes, there you were
Tears in your eyes
Standing by the door
Ready to walk
Ready to run
To another love
To another dream
That doesn't include me
Yes - You were standing there
Standing by the doorway of tears.

COMING HOME

It's been a long - long time
Since I've held you in my arms
Looked into your eyes
Told you that I love you
Yes - It's been a long - long time
Since we loved the nights away

Now you are coming home
Coming home to me
To these arms you know
Yes - you are coming home
To the one who loves you so
Yes - you are coming home
Coming home to me
Back in my heart
Back in my arms
Back where you belong

You went away
So long ago
To find yourself
To know your soul
To know the inner you
Yes - you went away
So long ago

Yet never once did I
Try to chase away
Chase away my love for you
Never once could I
Forget the love we had
The love we shared as one

Yes - It's been a long - long time
Since I've held you in my arms
Looked into your eyes
Told you I love you
Yes - It's been a long - long time
Since we loved the nights away

Now you are coming home
Coming home to me
To these arms you know
Yes - you are coming home
To the one who loves you so
Yes - you are coming home
Coming home to me
Back in my heart
Back in my arms
Back where you belong

I didn't want you
To go away
The way you did
So long ago

But I have come
To finally understand
Your need to find
The meaning of your life
And who you really are
And yes - I am happy now
Now that you have finally found
That I am where you belong
Yes - you are coming home
Coming home to me
To love our life away.

CALLED AWAY

You have held my hand
Through many risings of the sun
You have kissed my lips
With a passion before unknown
And you have shared your gifts
Through the many nights
When we were all alone
Yes, the love you gave
Throughout your life
Was more than I deserved

And that is why
In the deepest parts
Deepest parts of my nights
I cry myself to sleep
And that is why
I have learned to cry
A river of tears
Since you were called away
To a distant land
By a God never seen
Yes, you were called away
Away from me
To a paradise

That I will one day see
And though the wait may be long
Before we meet again
I will join you there
Before the memories die

There has never been
And there will never be
One as beautiful
As beautiful to me
There will never be
Another in my life
To share their love
As you had with me
Why He called you away
In the prime of love
I may never know
But I want you to know
That you'll be here
Forever in my heart
Forever in my soul

Yes - You've gone away
To a distant land
Far away from me
Yes - You've been called away
By a God unknown to me
To live eternally

In a land called Paradise
Now gone are the nights
When we shared our hearts
And loved away the nights
Yes - Gone are the days
Of sunshine forever in your eyes
Yes - Gone are the pleasures
That came from loving you.

A MOTHER'S LOVE

(Dedicated to my mother from her 11 children)

When our pains seemed too great to bear
And our sorrows seemed far greater
Than the sands upon the shore,
Like a bridge over troubled waters
You eased them with your love

When in our beds we lay
Too sick to raise our heads,
It was you who sat beside us
Gentle hands upon our face
And prayed us back to health

When the pains and sorrows
That life often freely brings
Would send us to our knees,
It was you who held out a hand
And gave us hope, love and faith

When our world came crashing down
And life seemed at its end,
It was you who took our burdens,
Took them deep within your bosom
Least we feel those pains again

And yes – even when we hurt you
As we children often did,
Never once did your love waiver
For you alone knew that only love
Would soon replace the raging storms

When voices barely heard cried out
No matter time of day or night,
You put aside your own troubled fears
And showed us that even rainbows
Can be seen through our tears

Yes – A mother's love is forever
Unconditional for us all
No love under the stars
Could be as everlasting
As the love you shared with us.

BEFORE THE EVENING DIES

The sun is soon to fall
Beyond the distant sky
Erasing yet another day
But before it goes
Before the memories pass
Before the evening dies
I need to take you in my arms
Pull you close to me
To let you know once more
How much I really love you
Before - Before the evening dies

Not a day goes by
That you're not on my mind
That my love for you
Doesn't grow by the hour
No could ever make me feel
This love I feel
So deep within my heart
And that is why
Before the evening dies
I want to pull you close

To let you know
How much I really love you
To let you know
Before the evening dies

Not a day goes by
That I don't feel blessed
To have you at my side
Many prayers I have prayed
At the end of a day
In thankfulness for you
For you are one of a kind
Always on my mind
Twenty-four hours a day
So before - the evening dies
I want to love you again
Yes before - Before the evening dies
I want to love you
I want to love you all over again.

A FATHER'S FAREWELL

(Dedicated to my Father ~ in my Father's voice)

Before I go
Before the angels call me home
I have a few words
I've always wanted to share

So before I go
Before the angels call me home
I just want you to know
From my heart and soul
That I've always loved you
Yes - It sometimes seemed
That I have been unfair
Not always able to share
In your life and your dreams
Yes - I know that it's true
That we didn't always agree
On what's right and what's wrong
And those angry words
We sometimes exchanged
For reasons unknown
But never once did I

Through those troubled times
Ever love you less
Than all my heart could give

So before I go
Before the angels call me home
I have a few words
I've always wanted to share

So before I go
Before the angels call me home
I just want you to know
From my heart and soul
That I've always loved you all
Yes - I've prayed everyday
That you would always be
The best you could be
That you would always seek
To be forever true
To the love God has given you
Yes - I have always prayed
That life would be kind
Until the end of time
Yes - I want you to live
With good memories
Of the love I tried to give

Yes - and I apologize
If I let you down
Or did you wrong
Somewhere along the way
And yes - I apologize
For all the many times
I never took the time
To say from my heart and soul
How much I loved you all

So now - before I'm gone
To that distant land
I can only hope and pray
That you will remember
The times I loved you so
Yes - Before I go
Before the angels call me home
I wanted you to know
From my heart and soul
That I've always loved you all
More than you could ever know
From deep within my soul
So before I go
Before the angels call me home
Let me say once more
From my heart and soul
That I've always loved you all.

BY MY SIDE

The times have not been easy
As I've made my way through life
For I have known pain so deep
That I wished my life
Was but a memory
And I remember still
All the lonely times
When I would try to hide
Try to hide from myself
Yes - Those were such lonely times
When I lost my soul
To the pleasures of the night
But now - Since you have come
Come into my life
And showed me love
I have never known pain

Never before have I
Known a love like yours
In all the years of my life
No one I have ever known
Has stood by my side
As you have with me
No one I have ever known

Has believed in me
As you have in me
And now I know
That my future is bright
And filled with peace and love
Knowing you are by my side

I have felt the kiss of death
When life lost its meaning
When you were unknown to me
I have felt the fires of hell
Before you came along
And lifted me up
Yes - I have tested fate
When my sight was blinded
By the tears in my eyes
But then you came along
And kissed the tears away
And I could finally see
The answer to my dreams
For with you by my side
No reasons have I to cry
No need to feel the pain
That loneliness always brings
For with you by my side
Tears are but a memory
For with you by my side
Loneliness lives no more

And lifted me up
Yes - I have tested fate
When my sight was blinded
By the tears in my eyes
But then you came along
And kissed the tears away
And I could finally see
The answer to my dreams
For with you by my side
No reasons have I to cry
No need to feel the pain
That loneliness always brings
For with you by my side
Tears are but a memory
For with you by my side
Loneliness lives no more.

A SILENT CRY

(Dedicated to Unborn Children)

A silent cry and unseen tears
Unknown whys and climbing fears
A touch of cold by faceless souls
The end I fear is near

Through love you gave me life
Your body warm - my home
So peaceful was my life
So secure I felt inside

And then I heard your fateful words
Little emotion did you show
And then I heard those chilling words
No longer will I grow

A silent cry and unseen tears
Unknown whys and climbing fears
A touch of cold by faceless souls
The end I fear is near

Why must you end it all
This God-given future bright
I want to stand so tall
To love and do what's right

Future doctor to save a life
A leader to guide the world
A lover to bring new life
A song to warm a heart

A silent cry and unseen tears
Unknown whys and climbing fears
A touch of cold by faceless souls
The end I fear is near
Futures great I'll never know
Steel cold reaching in on me
A surgeon's knife becomes my foe
A life of love I'll never know

Please say no before I go
Let love guide your mind
Give me hope and time to grow
And I'll give to all mankind

A silent cry and unseen tears
Unknown whys and climbing fears
A touch of cold by faceless souls
The end I fear is near

Why can't you hear the cries?
That comes from deep inside
Why can't you feel me move?
Anticipating life outside

But should you end my life
Before its natural time
I forever wish you peace of mind
As I send my love from above

May your God watch over you
Every day and every night
May he bring you lasting peace
And ease your troubled mind

A silent cry and unseen tears
Unknown whys and climbing fears
A touch of cold by faceless souls
The end I know is near
The end I fear is here.

IN THE NIGHT HE CAME

There was a time
When in my prime
I had it all
I could stand tall
A lovely wife
Children three
Money more
Than I could spend
Nothing more
Could I want or need

And then He came
In the night he came
Softly He whispered hello
Arise from your sleep
It's time to go
You've lived your life
So it's time to go

How could He come?
Upon the night
When my life
Was far from done
With a wife

And children three
Who He knows
Depend on me
I can't believe
My time is near
That I could fall
With His simple call

Looking back
At this life I've lived
Few regrets
Cross my mind
I've shared my life
With those who dared
I've given love
To those who cared
I had it all
I could stand tall

And then He came
Oh yes He came
When in my prime
Before my time
In the night He came
Softly He whispered hello
Arise from your sleep
It's time to go
You've lived your life
So it's time to go.

THE VOICES OF LOVE

Listen to the angels
Singing out with joy
Look upward to the heavens
Blessings raining down on us
Lift your eyes to the stars
Watch them dancing for us
Yes - All of this is ours
For we both have heard
The voices of love
Now we are as one
With rings exchanged
For we both have heard
The voices of love
Singing out
Singing out with love

We have found true love
In each other's arms
To last forever more
We knew it when
We looked within
Each other's eyes
And saw the look
Radiating from the heart

And we knew that look
Would bring us to this day
For the voices of love
We are ringing
Ringing in our hearts

No words can describe
The love we feel inside
On this special day
Where two hearts
Come together as one
And we promise love
Till death do us part
For we both have heard
The voices of love
Singing out to us
So we give our love
Our hearts and our souls
On this our wedding day

So listen to the angels
Singing out with joy
Look upward to the heavens
Blessings raining down on us
Lift your eyes to the stars
Watch them dancing for us
Yes - All of this is ours
For we both have heard

The voices of love
Now we are as one
With rings exchanged
For we both have heard
The voices of love
Singing out
Singing out with love
Yes - the voices
The voices of love.

LOVE - HOPE & PROMISES

The phone is silent without you
The nights are empty without you
But faith I will keep in time and you
For I believe in Love -
Love, Hope & Promises
For they are the essence of you

This tiny room I fear to leave each night
For the call from you I fear to miss
Only you can free me from this prison hell
For I believe in Love -
Love, Hope & Promises
That you will finally set me free

Your sparkling eyes have captured my heart
Skipping furiously into space
And you speak so softly from your heart
Now I believe in Love -
Love, Hope & Promises
For you are the sources of my dreams

There was a time when dreams were all I had
Looking for reality by way of you
Now my heart feels the caress of your love
For I believe in Love -
Love, Hope & Promises
For my dreams truly rest with you

The phone finally rings but it's not you
How long must the wait go on?
Before the voice I hear is yours?
But I believe in Love -
Love, Hope & Promises
For love is all one can give

Your smile is wide your laugh is real
Both I need to see and hear again
I know you'll want to ease this aching heart
For I believe in Love -
Love, Hope & Promises
That only you can make come true

How long is long enough to wait for you?
For the days seem like an eternity
But wait I must for the thrill of your unknowns
For I believe in Love -
Love, Hope & Promises
For your love is all I could want

Be kind to me and ease these lonely pains
Pains I hope you'll never feel
As happiness is all that I could hope for you
For I believe in Love -
Love, Hope & Promises
For your love is all I could want.

BROKEN PROMISES

Broken - broken promises
Telltale lies
Broken promises
A heart that cries
Broken promises
A soul that dies
That's what you've given me
That's what you've done to me
Broken promises
Broken promises by you

You promised love for the entire world to see
A wedding ring with tears I gave to thee
A future bright is all that I could see
And then you walked
Walked away from me
And then you walked
Walked away from me
And then you walked - from my heart

You promised life together you and me
Children many to be all they can be
A simple life with God and family
And then you turned

Turned away from me
And then you turned
Turned away from me
And then you turned - from my heart

Broken - broken promises
Telltale lies
Broken promises
A heart that cries
Broken promises
A soul that dies
That's what you've given me
That's what you've done to me
Broken promises
Broken promises by you

You promised wine to spice the love we shared
Nights so tender and hugs to show you cared
Sharing our souls and living life with a flair
And then you flew
Flew away from me
And then you flew
Flew away from me
And then you flew - from my heart

You promised truth to guide us thru life
Always striving to be the perfect wife
Seeking one life to last 'till the after-life
And then you lied

Lied before my eyes
And then you lied
Lied before my eyes
And then you lied - with your heart

Broken - broken promises
Telltale lies
Broken promises
A heart that cries
Broken promises
A soul that dies
That's what you've given me
That's what you've done to me
Broken promises
Broken promises by you

You promised joy for all eternity
A model life for everyone to see
Never loud words promising to agree
And then you left
Left me all alone
And then you left
Left me all alone
And then you left - with my heart

You promised hope for a life with one mate
We together making a lifetime date
Our souls as one for love with you was great

And then you hurt
Hurt until I cried
And then you hurt
Hurt until I cried
And then you hurt - 'till I died

Broken - broken promises
Telltale lies
Broken promises
A heart that cries
Broken promises
A soul that dies
That's what you've given me
That's what you've done to me
Broken promises
Broken promises by you

You promised all that life and love could crave
For only you I swore my love to save
For only you I will love to my grave
And then you fell
Fell away from me
And then you fell
Fell away from me
And then you fell - from my heart

You promised grace for love that knows no shame
A guiding light for love's eternal flame
Bringing peace least love remain untamed

And then you tore
Tore my love apart
And then you tore
Tore my love apart
And then you tore - away my heart

Broken - broken promises
Telltale lies
Broken promises
A heart that cries
Broken promises
A soul that dies
That's what you've given to me
That's what you've done to me
Broken promises
Broken promises by you.

DOORWAY OF TEARS

There you were
Standing by the door
Suitcase on the floor
Yes, there you were
Tears in your eyes
Standing by the door
Ready to walk
Ready to run
To another love
To another dream
That doesn't include me
Yes, you were standing there
Standing by the doorway of tears

Through the ups and downs
Despite all the pains
That came along our way
I never once gave up
On our vows of love
I never once gave up
Throughout all the storms
That has rocked our hearts
On our way through life
Yes - Despite the pains

From all the storms
You're still the only one
I'll ever want to love
Yes, the only one
To keep this flame alive
This flame that burns for you

But there you were
Standing by the door
Suitcase on the floor
Yes, there you were
Tears in your eyes
Standing by the door
Ready to walk
Ready to run
To another love
To another dream
That doesn't include me
Yes, you were standing there
Standing by the doorway of tears

When you walk out that door
I want you to know
That you are leaving behind
One lonely broken heart
That you are leaving behind
These shattered dreams
Lying on the floor

Lying beneath your feet
Yes, these shattered dreams
A broken heart
Given to known fears
At the doorway of tears

But there you were
Standing by the door
Suitcase on the floor
Yes, there you were
Tears in your eyes
Standing by the door
Ready to walk
Ready to run
To another love
To another dream
That doesn't include me
Yes - You were standing there
Standing by the doorway of tears.

VANITA IN MY DREAMS

Vanita - Take me in your arms
Vanita - Kiss away my tears
Vanita - Share with me your charms
Vanita - Chase away my fears
Answer all my dreams
End the nights as one
Let's love as though a team
Let's love in unison

Your voice I've never heard
Your face I've never seen
But the stories told by all
Speak of beauty deep within
And that's where love begins
Yes - that's where love begins

Will I ever touch your soul?
Only God will ever know
Is there room within your heart
For a man whose lost in dreams?
Or will the sorrows of my heart
Cause your love to turn away?
Cause your love to turn away?

Before the years turn me old
Let me come in from the cold
Please make our dreams as one
Let's leave the past far behind
Step boldly to tomorrow
And give our love a chance
Yes - give our love a chance

Vanita - take me in your arms
Vanita - kiss away my tears
Vanita - share with me your charms
Vanita - chase away my fears
Answer all my dreams
End the nights as one
Let's love as though a team
Let's love in unison

Yesterdays were filled with pain
Buried deep within my soul
Maybe you can bring the love
To wash away those pains
To cleanse my soul of memories
I would just as soon forget
I would just as soon forget

Your picture I do hold
In this mind I seldom know
Such beauty in your face
So tender are your eyes

Excitement through me runs
At the thought of loving you
At the thought of loving you

Forgive me for my dreams
But life is rushing by
And the thought of losing you
Would set my heart to cry
So take my hand in yours
And let our hearts be full
And let our hearts be full

Vanita - take me in your arms
Vanita - kiss away my tears
Vanita - share with me your charms
Vanita - chase away my fears
Answer all my dreams
End the nights as one
Let's love as though a team
Let's love in unison.

FROM A WINDOW

From a window high up in the sky
I see a world not meant for me
From a window high up in the sky
I witness love swiftly flying by

Reflections of a yesterday
Visions of no more today's
Endless thoughts of timeless days
Moonless nights and sightless eyes

My body stands with quiet ease
As my mind rolls forever on
I dreamt of endless rainbows
Finding only empty arms

From a window high up in the sky
I see a world not meant for me
From a window high up in the sky
I witness love swiftly flying by

Crying out on deafened ears
I prayed someday that love would hear
Hear the sound of loneliness
Beating from my empty heart

And so my life is told
As the pain has turned me cold
Dreams of endless lasting love
Replaced by a shattered heart

So from a window high up in the sky
Where the skies meet the clouds
A lonely figure leaps for love
Taking with him a lonely mind
Leaving behind bitter memories
Of endless love never found
Of endless love never found.

VISIONS OF LOVE

I've lived forever
With visions of love
Buried deep within my mind
I've lived a lifetime
With visions of love
And what true love
Ought to really be
I've sought out love
To quell this fire
Burning deep within my heart
To quell this fire
Raging out of control

I've sought out love
To bring new meaning
To this lonely world
I've come to know
I've sought out love
To erase the pains
I know too well
And then -

When I had given up on love
From the snow white clouds above
You came to me

You gave me life
You showed me what
Love was all about

Yes you came to me
Yes you gave me life
You brought reality
To these visions of love
You quelled this fire
Burning deep inside of me
You brought the light
To chase away
The darkness in my days

Yes - I have lived
With these visions of love
Dancing in my head
Playing games with my heart
Teasing my soul
And then -

You came to me
You brought me light
You gave me love
You filled these visions
With reality
You came to me
You brought me light

You gave me love
You filled these visions
With your nurturing warmth
You came to me
You gave me love.

UNVEILED MEMORIES

It was not so long ago
That the air was bitter cold
And white flakes of snow
Covered the barren ground
Yes - it was not so long ago
That you and I had shared a tear
And laughed at the past
That we held each other's hand
While wishing the past to last

Yes - it was not so long ago
That we shared our yesterdays
And memories known
By only you and I
Yes - we cherished the moments shared
And cried at the happier times
Remembering hugs so very tight

Yes - it was not so long ago
That our hearts were warmed
And our tears they flowed
With each unveiled memory
And now you're gone
To a distant shining star

Yes - to a better world
Beyond my reaching arms
And though the distance may be great
I want you my love to know
That your love is near
Every time I recall
The unveiled memories

As I lie here with my mind
In the stillness of the night
I can't help but regret
The many times I forgot
To tell you 'I love you'
And as I lie here awake
Lost deep in my thoughts
I can't help but recall
All the good times we had
But still I regret
That the love we had known
Must finally come home
Through unveiled memories.

UNTIL I MET YOU

I've been to places unseen
By all but the brave
I've lived out my youth
Living on the edge
And I've done some things
That even brought me shame
But I never found
No - I never knew
What love was all about
No - I never knew
What life could really give
Until I met you

Now my life has changed
In a thousand different ways
Now that you've won my heart
Now all things
I've done before
Mean nothing to me now
For what you have
What you possess
Is and will always be
More than I deserve
Yes - What you've given me

Is more than I deserve
For I never knew
What life could give?
What love was all about?
Until - yes until
Until I met you

The blessings given me
Come solely from the love
The love you've given me
There's been nothing at all
Nothing in my past
That could take the place
Or equal the thrill
Of being loved by you
No sweetness have I known
To match your kisses
Kisses sweet as wine
No - I never knew
What life could give
What love was all about?
Until - yes until
Until I met you

Yes - I've been to places unseen
By all but the brave
I've lived out my youth
Living on the edge

And I've done some things
That even brought shame
But I never found
No - I never knew
What love was all about?
No - I never knew
What life could really give
Until - yes until
Until I met you.

TOUCHED

Summer suns and winter winds
Have come and gone - once again
As quiet as the night
The rains and snows and bitter winds
Have left their mark - on everyone
With the passing of time
Yes - memories of seasons lost
Seasons come and gone - once again
Silently slipping from my mind

But memories that will never leave
Are of the love you share with me
For I have been touched
Every day I have been touched
Touched by the stars
Shining in your eyes
Touched by the warmth
Of your gentle body
Clinging tightly to mine
Touched by your smile
Easing all the pains
That creep into my days
Touched - Yes touched

Touched by the love
You so freely give
Deep into the nights

You've been everything
A man could ever want
More than I deserve
You've been there every moment
When I've needed a friend
And even during the rough times
Your hand was always there
There can never be another
Who can equal your touch?
Yes - the touch of love
That you possess
Has a hold on my heart
So let the seasons come and go
Cause I don't really care
For your touch is in my soul

Yes - The memories that will never leave
Are of the love you share with me
For I have been touched
Every day I have been touched
Touched by the stars
Shining in your eyes
Touched by the warmth

Of your gentle body
Clinging tightly to mine
Touched by your smile
Easing all the pains
That creep into my days
Touched - yes touched
Touched by the love
You so freely give
Deep into the nights.

TO KNOW WHO I AM

Honey - I can see
By the look in your eyes
That I am not here
Here by your side
It's just that I've gone
On a trip with my mind
Lost in my thoughts
Thinking of you
Of love - time and life
For there are those times
When I must escape
From what is at hand
To know who I am

Yes - to know
To know who I am
And what I've become
Yes - to know
To know who I am
And what you mean to me
And after I return
When my searching is done
I'm hoping you will be there
In love at my side

When I finally arrive
From who I am
Yes - from time to time
I must reflect alone
Reflect on you and me
To know who I am

I see the concern
Written on your face
When I seem far away
But I can only ask
That you worry not
For the dreams I chase
Are only in my mind
I will not wander far
Far from your side
I will not travel
From what I know
As long as you are here
And I shall return
With my love intact
As long as you remain
In love at my side

Yes - to know
To know who I am
And what I've become
Yes - to know

To know who I am
And what you mean to me
Is all that I ask
And after I return
When my searching is done
I'm hoping you will be there
When I finally arrive
From who I am
Yes - from time to time
I must reflect alone
Reflect on you and me
To know who I am.

TAKE ME BACK

Take me back
Oh, please my love
Please take me back
For I have learned
While looking for me
That the grass was not greener
In the arms of another
That the lips were not sweeter
When they were not yours

Yes, I have learned
Through leaving you
That my tomorrows are empty
Without you so near
Yes, I have learned
While looking for me
That the rainbows end
Would lead me to you

So, please take me back
I beg of you
Please take me back
And to you I promise

That I will never leave
Your loving arms again
Or cause you pain
Till the world is no more

I took with me
A part of you
That teased
My troubled mind
And nourished
My wandering heart
I set out bold
To find the gold
That was only in my mind
Which left me bitter cold

I took for granted
What you gave to me
All these many years
The loving nights
The warm embrace
The silent times
Shared as one
The sparkling eyes
The lips so sweet
The peaceful smiles
And knowing mind

The loving tears
The giving heart
But most of all
For your forgiving soul
And your belief in me

So, please take me back
Keep my love on track
Oh, take me back
I beg of you
For I have learned
While looking for me
That the grass was not greener
In the arms of another
That the lips were not sweeter
When they were not yours

Yes, I have learned
Through leaving you
That tomorrows are empty
Without you so near
Yes, I have learned
While looking for me
That the rainbows end
Would lead me to you
So, please take me back
I beg of you

Please take me back
And to you I promise
That I will never leave
Your loving arms again
Or cause you pain
Till the world is no more.

TAKE MY HAND

(A Wedding Song © **1971.** Go to michaelRjennings.com
to hear the actual song … click on Michael's music)

Take my hand my darling
And I'll lead you down
The road that leads to me - leads to me

Take my hand my love
And we'll walk forever
On the cotton - cotton clouds of love

May you never see a lonely day
Or spend a single night alone
May our love be as the song of time
That continues on and on - on and on

I'm just an ordinary person
Nothing special - no one grand
Until you look at me
Until you touch my hand
And then - I am everything

So take my name my darling
And you'll have my love
For a life - lifetime too

So take my heart my love
And I'll surely know
That it is safe - it is safe

May our love for each other be a guide
For all the world to see
May the love we feel grow stronger
As we live together day by day - day by day

I'm just an ordinary person
Nothing special - no one grand
Until you look at me
Until you touch my hand
And then - I am everything

So come - my beautiful love
And you'll never, never, never know
The end of time or love - the end of time or love.

TEARS ARE FOR SHARING

When you're feeling low
From a stressful day
Don't be afraid
To seek out a friend
Or someone you love
Don't be afraid
To reveal your tears
To unload your fears
For tears are for sharing

When you're feeling alone
With the weight of the world
Falling down on you
Don't be afraid
To call out a name
For they will come to you
They will ease your pains
No matter what it takes
So don't be afraid
To reveal your tears
To unload your tears
For tears are for sharing

There can be nothing worse
Than a lonely tear
Unseen and unheard
For there should never be
A time to hide
Your tears deep inside

For if you turn around
Someone can be found
To answer your prayers
So don't be afraid
To reveal your tears
To unload your fears
For tears are for sharing

Please feel free
To shed you tears
Unleash the pains inside
Free your heart and soul
With those who love you so
Let the tears freely flow
On a caring shoulder
That you know
Let the fears fade away
Before the rising sun
Of a brand-new day

Find a rainbow in the night
When the tears you cry
Are released to fly
On the shoulders of a friend
Or someone you love.
For tears are for sharing.

TENDER THOUGHTS AND YOU

Every time my mind runs free
When I'm all alone
No one to bother me
I tend to see the world
As it may never be
Living a fantasy
Unknown by man
Yes - Unknown by man
Except for me
For I'm the only one
Who knows the joys?
That comes from love
From being loved by you

And when my mind returns
To this real world
It always brings me back
To what is good
It brings me back
To tender thoughts and you
Yes - When I drift back
From unreality

That is when
I rediscover the whys
Of the joys in my life
That comes from you
That comes from love
That always comes
From tender thoughts and you

Yes - Tender thoughts
Tender thoughts and you
Tender - Most tender thoughts
Of love all around
Wherever you go
Wherever I am
Tender - soothing tender thoughts
Angel smiles in your eyes
Passions always running free
When you're alone with me
Yes - Tender thoughts
Tender thoughts and you

No matter where I go
Be it a distant star
Or alone in a car
My thoughts are never far
From tender thoughts and you
No matter the time of day
Or hour of night

You are always in my heart
For the love you give
Has always been
Far more than I deserve
And that is why
My wandering mind
Always returns to you
Returns to you
For the tender thoughts
That fills my mind
Are forever and ever of you
Yes - the tender thoughts
That invades my soul
No matter where I go

Yes - Tender thoughts
Tender thoughts and you
Tender - Most tender thoughts
Of love all around
Wherever you go
Wherever I am
Tender - soothing tender thoughts
Angel smiles in your eyes
Passions always running free
When you're alone with me
Yes - Tender thoughts
Tender thoughts and you.

THE POET SLEEPS

Fragrant candles burning brightly
Reveal eyes growing weary in the night
And as the moon shines its full light
It reveals the poet's unfinished lines

The lines upon his age-worn face
Tell the story of his broken life
Where love has come and gone again
Never quite filling that void inside

His poetry speaks of only love
As though love was life itself
But the sorrow that lies within the lines
Reveals a life devoid of real love

Every page speaks of an unnamed love
That has given inspiration to his words
And he even calls her by her names
Princess Love, Angel Eyes and God's special child

Written poems and even love filled songs
Have spoken the pages of his mind
Endless days and loveless nights
Were the price he's had to pay

Throughout life he sought but affection
But received only meaningless words
So with his tablet and well-worn quill
He seeks to express what life has denied

And as the moon slips behind the clouds
A solitary figure writes no more
His mind has finally found peace at last
Never to be denied love's pleasures again

His unfinished lines are now but a mystery
As are the unfound loves in his solitary past
And so this unknown poet of sorrow and pain
Shall remain a mystery unto his solitary grave.

THE FOUNTAINS OF MY LOVE

Every now and then
When I stop to reflect
On the goodness of my life
I can't help but think
And reminisce
On all that I've had
And all that I have
Every joy that I've known
All the treasures that I hold
Treasures both new and old
But most of all
When I reflect on my life
I can't help but think
Can't help but think of you
For you are the fountains
The fountain of my love

What I know of love
I have learned from you
All the joy in my life
Has come from knowing you
Every sunset I have seen

Is reflected in your eyes
Every smile on my face
Is brought about by you
All the love within my heart
I owe to only you
For you are the fountains
The fountain of my love

Can heaven be half as grand
As the love that we share?
Can the wonders of the world?
Match the love that we have?
Will the world ever know?
What I have found in you?
And all the riches in this world
Could never equal your love
For you have always been
And you will always be
The only one for me
For you are the fountains
The fountain of my love

Throughout all these years
I have been truly blessed
To have you at my side
And every day begins anew
So much love in my heart
For you are the fountains

That brings meaning to my life
For you are the fountains
Refreshing my mind
For you are the fountains
The fountain of my love
Yes - You are the fountain
The fountains of my love.

TAKE ME

From the corner of my eye
I caught you watching me
How can I tell you?
You need not be shy
For my heart has now been freed
No ring to tie me down
I'm as free as the wind
So take me if you please
For as you can see
I am all alone with me
No one near to hold
No one to call my own
No one calling me
Or knocking on my door
Yes - as you can see
I'm all alone
So take me
Take me if you please

I was in love before
To one more in love
In love with herself
Now that I have escaped
From the depths of hell

Now I need - need to find
Some one new to love
Some one new to return
To return my love

Now that I've noticed you
Staring straight at me
Will you move my way?
Will you dare to say?
What's on your mind
What lies in your heart?
Please come to me
Take me if you please
For I am all alone
No one near to hold
No one to call my own
No one calling me
Or knocking on my door
Yes - As you can see
I am all alone with me
So take me
Take me if you please.

STORYBOOK LOVE

Every time I look at you
I see the answer to my dreams
Every time I look your way
I see the butterflies
Dancing halos on your head
Every time that you are near
My heart skips a beat
Yes - every time
I look your way
The stars are in your eyes
Yes - A storybook love
Is what I have
It's what I have in you

Each chapter of my life
Is like a book
Happy endings everyone
For the love you give
Is more than anyone
Could ever write about
A Cinderella kind of love
That lives forever in the mind
Each chapter moves along
Where your kind of love

Is like a storybook love
That last 'till the end of time
Yes - 'Till the end of time
Our love will last
For ours is a storybook
A storybook kind of love

Time has been good to us
As we've shared our love
Through sometimes troubled times
But back we came
For more of the same
That has kept us in love
For you have been
And will always be
The storybook love of my life
Yes - You will always be
The only love I'll know
'Till the final chapter is told
In the storybook of love
The storybook
The storybook of love

Every time I look at you
I see the answer to my dreams
Every time I look your way
I see the butterflies
Dancing halos on your head

Every time that you are near
My heart skips a beat
Yes - every time
I look your way
The stars are in your eyes
Yes - A storybook love
Is what I have
It's what I have in you.

SPACE - TIME & WE

How often have we heard?
How often have we felt?
That we need some space
We need some time
To find the hidden we
Yes - We need our space
We need our time
To find meaning in our lives

We all need our space
To look outside ourselves
To bring reason to our souls
Yes - We need our time
To travel tomorrows past
To seek secrets known to none

Yes - We need our space
The space to walk
To unknown dreams
We need our time
The time to find
The deepest parts of us

Like a tide rushing out
A seagull gliding out to sea
We all need to back away
And take a thoughtful look
We all need to take the time
To reflect on where we've been
For by knowing where we've been
The better will it be
In knowing where we want to be.

BOOTS ON A CROSS

(Go to michaelRjennings.com to hear the actual song. Click on Michael's music)

While you're out burning flags
Covered by a flag I'll be
Protesting wars you'll see
I've become a silent memory

When your freedoms are at risk
And our country is at war
You can always count on me
To lead you through freedom's door.

Take me home
Take me home
Place my boots upon the cross
To a place that I'll call home
On this land where freedom reigns
No longer will I roam

It's been a long, long journey home
But here I am at last
In my new home of pine and stone
N'eath the cold hard ground and grass

I can hear the whisper of the leaves
As angels lift me up
To a world unknown to you
As I touch the face of God above

Take me home
Take me home
Place my boots upon the cross
To a place that I'll call home
On this land where freedom reigns
No longer will I roam

With family and friends nearby
Saying their final goodbyes
I once again would give my life
To our country where freedom lies

As I shed my blood for you
And took the final fall
For you to freely love again
While I... hear my... final call

Take me home
Take me home
Place my boots upon the cross
To a place that I'll call home
On this land where freedom reigns
No longer will I roam

Take me home
Take me home
Place my boots upon the cross
To a place that I'll call home
On this land where freedom reigns
No longer will I roam.

ARTHUR'S LEGACY

(Dedicated to the Memory of Arthur Robert Ashe Jr)
(1943-1993)

Arthur - We'll miss you so
For the love you shared with us
Arthur - We'll miss you too
For your visions and your dreams
Arthur - We wish you well
On your journey to your dreams
Arthur - It's a better world
You left behind
Because you deeply cared
And Arthur - May your legacy
Forever grow
Upon awakening souls
Arthur - Arthur
We will miss - miss you so

Arthur - Life for you
Was rich with love
Shared with those you touched
And those you never knew
Arthur - Through your quiet voice
You sought to open half closed eyes

And enlighten darkened minds
Yes - Enlighten minds
As you traveled life
Down dark and rocky roads

Arthur - You heard the cries
Of troubled souls
Seeking only to be free
You traveled the worldwide
Speaking out on deafened ears
You witnessed blood upon the ground
Where our brothers were beat down
But onward did you march
Knowing God would lead the way
To a future better day

Arthur - We'll miss you so
For the love you shared with us
Arthur - We'll miss you too
For your visions and your dreams
Arthur - We wish you well
On your journey to those dreams
Arthur - It's a better world
You left behind
Because you deeply cared
And Arthur - May your legacy
Forever grow

Upon awakening souls
Arthur - Arthur
We will miss - miss you so

Arthur - You were set free
When you dared to share
Convictions of your heart
And Arthur
We will remember that
You held your head up high
When those before you sought
To crush your soul-felt pride
And keep you in a world
Where your soul must always hide

Arthur - you are gone from us
To a better - richer life
And Arthur
We are richer too
For your spirit left behind
To rest within our souls
And light our darkest nights
Yes Arthur
We are richer too
For your visions shared
And dreams of we
That all men shall live free

Yes Arthur
We will miss you so
For the love you shared with us
Yes Arthur
We will miss you too
For your visions and your dreams
Yes Arthur - We wish you speed
On your journey to those dreams
Arthur - It's a better world
You left behind
Because you deeply cared
And Arthur - May your legacy
Forever grow
Upon awakening souls
Upon awakening souls.

GONE ARE
THE MOMENTS

Gone are the moments
When smiles in your eyes
Gone are the moments
When happy tears you cried
Gone are the moments
When simple were your dreams
Gone are the moments
When you heart you shared with me
Gone are the moments
When love did reign supreme
Yes gone - yes gone
Yes gone are the moments of love

I don't know when it came
But without a sound it came
The day when your love was no more
And now - as I sit alone
I only wish I knew
What pulled you away?
Was it time?
Was it fate?
Was it living life?

At too fast a pace?
Was it not knowing?
What tomorrows bring?
Or hanging on to long
To unfilled dreams?
I wish I knew
Yes dear - I wish I knew

For gone are the moments
When smiles in your eyes
Gone are the moments
When happy tears you cried
Yes - gone are the moments
When your heart you shared with me
Gone are the moments
When love did reign supreme
Yes gone - yes gone
Yes gone are the moments of love

I remember well
The love we had
Reaching far beyond the stars
I remember when
You loved me more
Than all the riches in the world
I remember well
The star-kissed nights
We shared till the rising sun

And yes - I remember when
Your heart you gave
For me to love and keep

But now
Gone are the moments
When smiles in your eyes
Gone are the moments
When happy tears you cried
Gone are the moments
When simple were your dreams
Yes - gone are the moments
When your heart you shared with me
Gone are the moments
When love did reign supreme
Yes gone - yes gone
Yes gone are the moments of love.

CITY OF ANGELS

City of angels
Whisper to me
Tell me your secrets
Of why your people are free

You have it all
With your winds gently blowing
Ever-lasting sun
And minds ever flowing

Whispering winds
Blowing gently from the sea
Sapphire skies so blue
For all the world to see
Where dreams can come true

City of Angeles
You'll always be my home
No matter where I live
No matter where I roam
You will always give me
A place ... for me to call home

Even though one walks in darkness
The City of Angels will give you light
Where dreams are born
For the likes of you and me

Pursuing the wind
Seeing the last light of day
Where one can see
The rainbows thru the rains

City of Angeles
You'll always be my home
No matter where I live
No matter where I roam
You will always give me
A place … for me to call home

You welcomed all from distant shores
People wanting to be free
May the cries of your people
Be answered without haste

The city will release you
Knowing that you will return.

A LADY BY DAY
(A Lover By Night)

She's a lady by day
A lover by night
And I am constantly high
When she's here at my side
Oh yes it is sweet
Watching heads turn around
As we walk down the street
And I haven't a care
For only me does she care
For she's a lady by day
A lover by night
This lady's in love with me

How lucky I am
To be holding her hand
For I know she is mine
And we will dance in the sand
Till the sun disappears
And the stars shine bright
Then like angels I'll hear
Her voice pleading softly to me
Now is the time
To return to the night
And do what lovers do

Yes, she's a lady by day
A lover by night
I am constantly high
When she's here at my side
Oh yes it is sweet
Watching heads turn around

As we walk down the street
But I haven't a care
For only me does she care
For, she's a lady by day
A lover by night
This lady's in love with me

With her head held high
She tackles the day
Moving with ease of grace
Though she works with the rich
I know she'll return
When the moon grows anew
For I know in my heart
That the love we have shared
Is on her mind
And thoughts of the night
Will bring her home to me

Yes, she's a lady by day
A lover by night
I am constantly high

When she's here by my side
Oh yes it is sweet
Watching heads turn around
As we walk down the street
But I haven't a care
For, she's a lady by day
A lover by night
This lady's in love with me
Yes, this lady's in love with me.

WHEN YOU SAY YES

The passions burn inside
From needing your love
From wanting to taste
Your sweet tenderness
Yes - The passions within
Are yearning to be free
Forever free for me
To devote my life
To loving only you
But the passions deep
Can only run free
When you say yes
To forever loving me
Yes - When you say yes
To loving only me

And when you say yes
To loving only me
Lightning will brighten
The nighttime skies
And angels will sing out
In perfect harmony
Thunder will roar across
The cloud-less blue sky

And lonely souls will arise
From their darkened graves
The moment you say yes
To forever loving me
Yes - When you say yes
To loving only me

All of this
Will come to be
When you say yes
To forever loving me
Yes all of this
And so much more
Will come to be
When you say yes
To forever loving me
Yes - When you say yes
To loving only me

Everything we do
We do together as one
Each and every day
We whisper 'I love yous'
Each and every night
We share our dreams
Of says yet to come
And all the while

The passions we feel
Could fill the seven seas
For the love we know
Keeps building inside
Like a volcano unleashed
And that my dear
Is why I need to hear?
To hear you say yes
For that simple word
Is all I need
To make my future complete

And when you say yes
To loving only me
Lightning will brighten
The nighttime skies
And angels will sing out
In perfect harmony
Thunder will roar across

The cloud-less blue sky
And lonely souls will arise
From their darkened graves
The moment you say yes
To forever loving me
Yes - When you say yes
To loving only me

All of this
Will come to be
When you say yes
To forever loving me
Yes all of this
And so much more
Will come to be
When you say yes
To forever loving me
Yes - When you say yes
To loving only me.

WHERE ONCE I COULD SEE

Where once I could see
I now only sense
The river running free
Racing quickly on its way
To meet the salty sea
Where once I could see
I now only sense
The blooming cherry trees
The fragrance of the rose
Ripening fruit upon the trees
Now that sight is gone from me

Where once I could see
I now only sense
The winds whistling thru the trees
Flowers honey for the bees
Bringing sweetness to you and me
Where once I could see
I now only sense
Lovers walking on the sand
Side by side holding hands
With tomorrow's on their minds
Now that sight is gone from me

Where once I could see
I now only sense
A smile on a face
The winners in a race
A chair out of place

Where once I could see
I now only sense
That love is all around
Firmly rooted on the ground
For those who care to share
Now that sight is gone from me

Where once I could see
I now only sense
The warmth of the sun
The glow of the moon
The presence of the stars
Where once I could see
I now only sense
A meal cooking slow
Strangers walking by
Geese flying low
Now that sight is gone from me
Yes - The sights I used to love
Are gone forever from my eyes

From: The Unpublished Musical, **Blind Love**
Lyrics/Play: Michael Jennings

ANOTHER DAY
WILL COME

I have heard you say
So many times
Busy are your lives
You need your space and time
Quiet moments to yourselves
You need to get away
From your harried days
Escape unto yourselves
Yes - I understand
The needs you have
To be alone
Without me around
And because -
I love you both
I will slip away
And wait my time
For another day will come

But that's okay daddy
Don't you worry mommy
I will be okay
For another day will come

Yes - Another day
Will come along
When you can be here
To watch me shine
Shine like the sun
Run like the wind
Soar like an eagle
Floating on the wind

Yes - Another day
Will come along
When you can see
See me score a run
Be an angel in a play
Holding hands with a friend
Or shedding a tear
When that friend moves away
But that's okay daddy
Don't you worry mommy
I will be okay
For another day will come
Yes - Another day
Another day will come

I've come to learn
Though still so young
To hide the tears
I cry inside

And in many ways
I have grown old
From growing alone
But I don't mind
For I love you both
And I understand
The needs you feel
To live a free life
To go when you want
And where you want
To enjoy life
To do as you please
Unencumbered by me
A mistake from your past

But that's okay daddy
Don't' you worry mommy
I will be okay
For another day will come

Yes - Another day
Will come along
When you can be here
To watch me shine
Shine like the sun
Run like the wind
Soar like an eagle
Floating on the wind

Yes - Another day
Will come along
When you can see
See me score a run
Be an angel in a play
Holding hands with a friend
Or shedding a tear
When that friend moves away
But that's okay daddy
Don't you worry mommy
I will be okay
For another day will come
Yes - Another day
Another day will come.

From: The Unpublished Musical, **Blind Love**
Lyrics/Play: Michael Jennings

WHO ARE YOU?

Who are you?
That you have
Such a hold on me
Who are you?
That you know
What you want
That you know
Who you are
Who are you?
That when you wish
Upon a star
Your wishes come true
Who are you?
That I would give
Give all I possess
Just to be a part
Be a part
A part of you

I've watched you over time
With a yearning in my heart
To be a part of you
To hold your hand
To take you in my arms

To love only you
Liked I've never loved
Loved anyone before
Who are you?
That only you
Could have such a hold on me

Who are you?
That when you walk
The rains do stop
Who are you?
That there is always
A full moon over you
Yes - Who are you?
That children never cry
When held by you
Who are you?
That roses open up
Whenever you walk by
Yes - Who are you?
That you're always on my mind
Always in my heart
Each and every day
Every day of my life

I've watched you over time
With a yearning in my heart
To be a part of you

To hold my hand
To take you in my arms
To love only you
Like I've never loved
Loved anyone before
Who are you?
That only you
Could have such a hold on me.

YOU'VE GOT TO FEEL
THE LOVE

If you feel the love
Then you know there's love
If you feel the love
Deep within your heart
Within your mind
Within your soul
Then you know there's love
Yes, there's really love
If you feel the love

There are the outward signs
That we know so well
"The I love yous"
The embraces warm
Kisses often shared
Walking hand in hand

But, to know there's really love
You've got to feel the love
Deep within your heart
Within your mind
Within your soul

Yes, to really know there's love
You've got to feel the love

Love cannot be bought
Turned off or on
Hidden away
Stored in a chest
Held in your hand
Or found in a book

Yes, to know there's really love
You've got to feel the love
Deep within your heart
Within your mind
Within your soul
Yes, to really know there's love
You've got to feel the love
You've got to feel the love.

From: The Unpublished Musical, **Blind Love**
Lyrics/Play: Michael Jennings

PASSIONS UNFOLDING

The innocence of youth
I watch from so near
In the flesh of my son
All the words I speak
He hears and obeys
Without questioning why

Seventeen though he be
To me he belongs
In his heart and his soul.
The closeness we know
Will never grow old
For as long as live

No sooner this said
Then a lassy he finds
And he cast me aside.
What could she possess?
That I haven't got
Or could buy for him soon

Then my own youth flashed
To reveal what caused me
To forsake my own dad.

I'm afraid to admit
The truth that I know
About my son and his gal

His passions are unfolding
For someone other than I
While I sadly look on.
Her supple breast enticing
And her lips the taste of honey
Have replaced me in his mind

Passions unfolding
Before me this day
Passions unfolding
No more can say
Passions unfolding
A son I have lost
To a woman that's got
What I never could give.

www.ingramcontent.com/pod-product-compliance
Lightning Source LLC
Chambersburg PA
CBHW060439130626
46555CB00005B/2430